To Gianna and Lydia
—JB

To my father
—LB

SIMON & SCHUSTER BOOKS FOR YOUNG READERS
1230 Avenue of the Americas, New York, New York 10020
Text copyright © 1994 by James Berry
Illustrations copyright © 1994 by Louise Brierley
Originally published in Great Britain in 1994 by Hamish Hamilton Ltd.
First American Edition, 1994. All rights reserved including the right of
reproduction in whole or in part in any form.
SIMON & SCHUSTER BOOKS FOR YOUNG READERS is a trademark
of Simon & Schuster. Typography design by David Neuhaus.
The text for this book is set in 17-point Bembo. The illustrations were
done in watercolor. Manufactured in Belgium.

10 9 8 7 6 5 4 3 2 1

Library of Congress Catalog Card Number: 93-87671

ISBN: 0-671-89446-3

Celebration Song

A Poem by James Berry

Illustrated by Louise Brierley

Simon & Schuster Books for Young Readers
Published by Simon & Schuster
New York London Toronto Sydney Tokyo Singapore

Your born-day is a happening day.
And, one year old today,
all day, I feel a celebration.
Everywhere is alive in jubilation.
All, O, all say, welcome!

And little eyes on me
light up lights in me
in choral songs,
in drums, flutes, and cymbals,
in a world praiseful and joyful.

Singing dogs bang tins.

Cows play violins.

Hounds dance with foxes.

Lions dance

Snakes and snakes

dance with mongooses.

Wind dances palm trees,
groups of children sing.
All the trees sway and swing.

Fields and fields of animals dance.

with lambs.

Elephants beat drums.

With only one reason
today, all out of season
flame trees blaze in blooms.

Your born-day is a happening day:
a caller with good news,
a day of celebration,
a day of jubilation.

But, baby, now — go to sleep.
Baby Jesus, go to sleep.
I'll tell you your *own own* story.
First — how you began.

You came here well announced.
In one year, you have caused
fears, visions, parables,
and the calling of councils.

Long before your coming
we had strange happenings.
A mystery messenger said
you would come to stay,

I should be your mother,
I should name you, Jesus.
In silence, in wonder,
afraid to say yes,
I knew I saw you, my Jesus.

You were born so very quietly
and so very very simply,
laid in a cattle-feeding trough,
wrapped in plain cloth.
But in a grand company,
messengers with no address
announced you to shepherds.

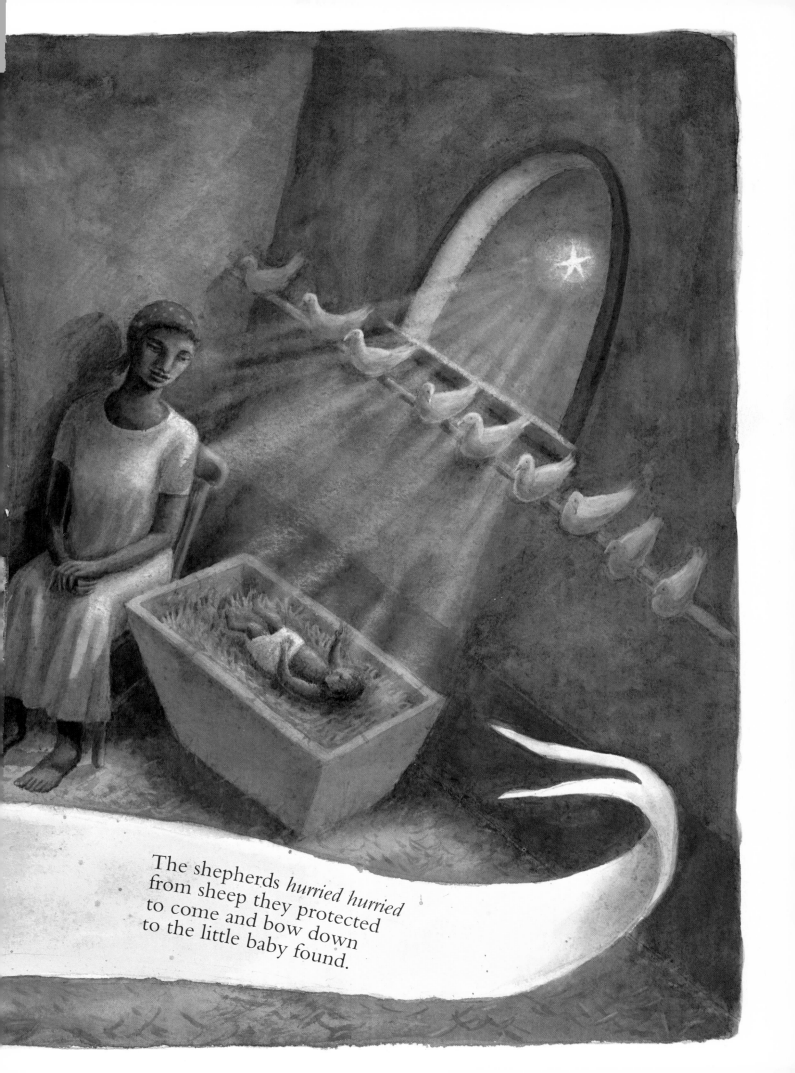

The shepherds *hurried hurried*
from sheep they protected
to come and bow down
to the little baby found.

Then, knowing your secret fame,
wise men, three astrologers
from a far country, came,
guided by a star,
to let your eyes meet theirs.

And there, over our roof,
the stopped star was the sign
to meet here and come in.

The visitors bowed down to you.
With their many respects
they gave you their gifts
and left you sleeping.

Your born-day is a happening day.
All day I feel a celebration,
everywhere alive in jubilation.

You tried to open my eyes
yesterday while I dozed,
not liking them closed.

Busy little hands troublesome:
they try to grasp my mouth,
my nose, eyes — I mock shout!

Out of bed with me today —
happiness! All day
music is in all of sky in my head.

Animals, people, trees
all say: first child
we want you for God's own child.

In the sea the fishes
all dance —
big fish, small fish, striped fish, plain fish —
in a leaping out-and-in dance,
in a leaping out-and-in dance,
in one all-day together wish.

All birds fill the sky
singing, flying in display
crisscrossed, this way and that way.

Your born-day is a happening day:
a caller with good news,
a day of celebration,
a day of jubilation.

Your born-day makes bells ring,
makes children and choirs sing,
brings strangers from near and far,
makes me feel afraid,
yet feel a joy without dread.

When you're grown up, and a man,
what will happen, happen then?
What will happen, Jesus?
What will happen to you, me, us?

Yet, also, I ask this:
when your childhood has gone —
my mothering long done —
will your day still be one
long long celebration day?